Also by Ellis Sharp

**Novels**

*The Dump*
*Unbelievable Things*
*Walthamstow Central*
*Intolerable Tongues*
*To Wetumpka*
*Lamees Najim*
*The Orwell Girl*
*Neglected Writer*
*What Vronsky Did Next*
*Twenty-Twenty*

**Short Fiction**

*The Aleppo Button*
*Lenin's Trousers*
(with Mac Daly) *Engels on Video*
*To Wanstonia*
*Driving My Baby Back Home*
*Aria Fritta*
*Quin Again and other stories*
*Dead Iraqis: Selected Short Stories*

**Non-Fiction**

*Sharply Critical*

ELLIS SHARP

# ALICE IN VENICE

Zoilus Press

A Zoilus Press paperback
First published in Great Britain by Zoilus Press in 2022

© Ellis Sharp 2022

All photographs including the cover image,
© Ellis Sharp 2022

A CIP catalogue record for this book is available from the
British Library.

ISBN 9781838489823

Cover design by The Ever-Shifting Subject
Typeset by Electrograd


ZOILUS PRESS
York, England

ALICE IN VENICE

# 1

*Sempre diretto!* Chop, chop! At the top – dark, hard to see, its symmetries obscure – of the derelict palazzo. That location where the shuddering loud fatal flashing reverberating blood-drenched terrible assault occurs. The landing steps of the church at the very end, where the funeral takes place. That other church where John Baxter – Donald Sutherland – has the accident which might have sent him tumbling to his death. These are the places Alice most wants to visit. There are fan websites which identify the names and locations of these places. Later, her preliminary research done, Alice goes to Stanfords in Covent Garden. There she buys their biggest and best map of Venice. She locates the three sites. There are others to be sought out along the way. The empty hotel where Sutherland and Christie, the last visitors, are staying. The restaurant where Laura Baxter faints; where she first encounters the two women. The canal basin where the corpse of a woman is hauled dripping from the depths. That place where the canal splits into two waterways, where Baxter and his wife are forced to stop. Where the investigating officer stands on a balcony, observing. Those water-lapped steps where Sutherland sees a doll. The café where he waits while Laura goes off to see the two weird women. The agonized statue in the park which overlooks Julie Christie as she walks past with those two disturbing companions, Clelia Matania and Hilary Mason. Alice owes it to Militká to find these places. They went to see the movie years after it was released, at the radical low-price cinema in Chinatown. We will go to Venice together, Militká said. We will find those locations. Yes, Alice said. We will. But they never did. Militká died. And now here she is, Alice, in Venice. But not with Militká. She is with a sexy young Frenchman instead. Alain. It all happened unexpectedly. She was planning on ending up here, she had her map, but she was going to Florence first. Now Florence is off the itinerary. She doesn't have the time. She has to be in Alphabet City by the 13th. No matter. She can go to Florence another year. Perhaps she will marry and go there with a husband. A strange word, *husband*. She supposes she'll end up with one, eventually. But not Mark. No, Mark is toast. She has other options. But no rush. No one should marry before they are thirty-five. Poor Militká. Did she jump or was she pushed? Impossible to know. Alice will never understand why she chained herself to that Polish lump. He appeared affable but then so did Jeremy Bamber. You never know with people. There are depths in everyone. Sediments, bitterness, rage. Lust. Greed. The furies. Malice in all its glittering aspects. A smile is like the tip of a glacier. But enough of these banal reflections. Alice prefers to look at herself in the mirror. She raises her wine glass. She is still in good shape, still highly desirable. Cheers! She is drinking too much, as always. Why in hell not? She's tired. She's very tired. The world is ending. This planet is screwed. She wants to say goodbye. Enough, enough. In London, years earlier, she went with Militká to Waterloo station. They caught a stopping train to Esher. In the listings in *Time Out* there was a cinema showing *The Man Who Fell to Earth*. They detrained and walked there. It was not too far from the station. Long since demolished. An afternoon performance. The cinema almost empty. On the row behind two men who gabbled. Militká sprang up, hissed at them to BE QUIET. They obeyed. Militká angry was a sight to behold etc. She was the same at the opera. During *The Queen of Spades* a man in the row in front fell asleep. He began snoring. Militká prodded him awake with her parasol. BE QUIET. The oaf obeyed. She was delicious, Militká. She had a lover, a young Englishman. But she died a long time ago. And now Alice is in Venice, remembering. It is November. *November!* They meet by chance in Prague, at Kafka's grave. Later they go for a drink. Alain has black curly hair, a trim moustache. Normally Alice does not like men with moustaches. But Alain, apart from his facial blemish, is handsome. Slim, smart-casual, amusing. Thirtyish. Twinkly eyes. Cultured. She approves his taste in fiction and cinema. Hell, Alice is in the mood for a new adventure. A brief encounter. Some careless carefree unanchored sex. And Alain, thankfully, makes no mention of Grace Slick. She is tired of men who do that, thinking they are the first to impress her with their wit, thinking that she will be charmed and delighted. They walk, she and Alain, hand in dry hand back to her hotel. He stays the night. When they have sex – straightaway, then half an hour later, then again in the drowsy dawn – he is attentive, energetic, not too talkative. The pleasures are intense, satisfying. At breakfast he invites her to accompany him to Venice for a few days. He explains. He works some of the time, especially in the winter, as a waiter in Paris. The money is much better than you might imagine. In the summer he works at a restaurant in Biarritz. But he has a second occupation. He sells rare books. What kind? He grins. His eyes are greenish-black. Erotic books. Old ones. He has three for sale and he has five well-heeled buyers in Venice who are interested. He has them in his rucksack, very carefully wrapped. The rucksack goes with him everywhere – to breakfast, to a stranger's room, to a vaporetto. And so they depart – off on their great adventure. Alain, fluent in Italian, reserves them a room at the Hotel dei Dragomanni, Calle Dose da Ponte, 2711, Sestire San Marco, 30124, Venezia. When they arrive he asks to borrow her little Canon camera. They are in the elevator. Why? "For photograph." *Click!* The first memento.

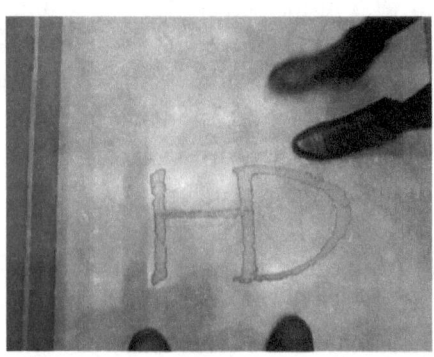

# 2

"I love you," Alain says. "I desire you." Alice says nothing. She goes over to the window. A black cat walks down the alley below. It is the first and the last cat she will see in Venice. There is a question that keeps her awake in the darkness. But now is not the moment to ask it. Perhaps the moment will never arrive. A glass of Valpolicella. Is that what she needs? A light rain is falling. Something happened today. "You must have noticed..." She lets the sentence fade out. Alain stays silent. In less than an hour and a half... "I'm seeing you for the first time." Alain strokes her arm. "Life is a confusion." He lies down on the bed. "Where am I going now?" His eyes are closed. Their two masks dangle from a hook by the big gilt-framed mirror. Nothing moves. No one speaks. Faint sounds are now heard. Papers being handled. A distant swaddled cough. The thin yapping of a faraway dog. An English voice, masculine, softly saying Primo, Secondo, Terzo...

# 3

That inexorable drum. The din of ringing bells. The blood. Brighter than you imagined blood could ever be. "I read in zigzags." After the miscarriage you needed to get away. A few days on your own. To sort yourself out. You didn't want to be with Mark. You didn't even want to see Mark. Besides, who was Mark – really? Faraway chimes. Alice pulls herself free. She moves away, stickily. "I see somebody now. But he's coming very slowly." What curious attitudes. It seems as if Alain has made up his mind to follow her. In the alley below three women and a man are talking with a polite animation. Now they are gone. Mist drifts in rolls from the Grand Canal. Alice is sitting in the chair between the hotel room door and the table. She is naked. "No," Alain whispers. "This night could not exist without you." Alice produces a mournful smile. "I answered you." "What did you tell him?" "I said drowned in the lake. Do you mind?" "No, why should I?" The peignoir was closed. "Can you help me? You haven't answered." What had he been doing all morning long? The excitement mounted. "Uno... due... tre." There was laughter and hand-clapping. For the time being there was no cause for excessive concern. "Are you cold?" "Not too cold." The route she chooses is in reality far from straight. As if such things were possible anyway in this terrain. Alain kisses her hands. He says it's too late now for knowledge. For a long while they are silent. Later, in a bar not far from the cathedral where Julie Christie lights six candles, a waiter brings them coffee. "I slept so well," Alice confesses. Outside the November mist is thickening again. It is like being in an Antonioni movie. "Happiness is not geometrical." That is what the woman said to the man on the Zattere quay. "When you reach the second or third sentence, you should tear this letter up!" "Really? Do you really mean that? Or are you just saying it to impress me?" "Well, you know what they say." "What do they say?" "Don't go looking for soap-bubbles in a field of wheat."

# 4

Alice goes first to the church where it ended. The place where the mourners step off the funeral barge and walk into the dark interior. It is the same but different, this landing stage. She goes alone. Alain has gone off to meet someone "on business". She knows better than to ask what that might be. She does not need to know. What a character he is! Yes, this is the place. The funeral barge bursting out from a side canal. The surge of music. The disembarking mourners. The credits beginning to roll.

# 5

Alain's book dealing is a front for his real trade. Inside those hollowed-out books is the finest crystal meth that Venetian money can buy. Alain only accepts US dollars, in cash. He has a doctorate in organic chemistry. He has a fortune stashed away in Bitcoin. He plans to retire at forty and live in Utah. He has watched *Breaking Bad* three times. Soon it will be time for a fourth viewing. He knows Alice will not betray him. His trust in her is absolute. It is because she does not take drugs. She cannot be weakened that way. Fine wines are her only tipple. She loathes whisky, gin, spirits in general. Alain knows all the top Venetian families. Not necessarily the parents. It's the children who purchase. They know him. He has a reputation. He is reliable. He isn't flash. Not for him fast cars or private jets. He uses public transport. He checks into middle-range hotels. He doesn't attract attention. Alain puts two sticks of gum into his mouth. His breath always smells of peppermint. It is better than halitosis. But it can get tiresome. In New York, he tells her, he always eats at The Plaza. Oyster stew with cream. And afterwards... The plots he could weave, the tales he could tell! A born spinner. So she imagines, as she strolls across the famous square. Where is he now, this phantom of her mind? He is probably standing at the opposite side of the room, over by the window. He is looking down at a black cat which is walking purposefully along the alley, heading for the Grand Canal. Soon it will be nightfall. A strange bang like a shot pierces the dusk. Alice hears a sudden surge of voices. The language sounds like Russian. Whatever they are saying they are saying it with passion. Three voices. Two women and a man. Now one of the women is laughing. And now they move off, talking more quietly now. Gone. "We could leave together if you like," Alice suggests. But Alain does not think that is a good idea. He is fearful that the cops are on to him. He kisses her hands. "You must have fallen asleep again." "I expect so. It is more than possible." "I would like to distort it even more." "Is that wise? Your readers..." "My readers do not yet exist, chérie." "Then you must make them understand..." "That night on the Lido..." "I understand." "I hope you do. Because first you are bewildered. And then you love. And then you suffer." "Is that a quotation? It sounds like a quotation." "That depends. Do they know I am here?" "A saxophone, I believe." "Where are you going?" "Nowhere." "I only give orders and obey orders." "Who will you importune next with your aberrations?" By eleven at night the crowds in the square have gone. You walk over to where Alain and Ernest Hemingway are waiting. Alain is a huge Hemingway fan, which Alice is not. Alain tells her the story. His eyes twinkle under the electric light. "Hemingway he arrive for first time in Venice in 1948. Since that times, he keep coming back there – here – and he start to write again after ten years of stop." Silence. Alice nods. She feels some kind of gesture is required to keep the prose lubricated. "During one of his stay Hemingway he fall in love with the noble 19-year-old Adriana Ivancich." Older man, younger woman, old story. La peau douce. "Relations grow between them, even though never carnal." Alain winks.

"Except, of course, in pages of his book. The thirty-year difference of age and wife always prevents those from concretizing what they feel." "You don't say." *I will leave my heart here*, Hemingway said, meaning Venice. But Alice is unable to locate that withered organ. Her own drumming pump isn't left in this watery city, it must be said. *Must?* But if it was, she would deposit it with the other plastic sacks of refuse piled around the old closed wells which protrude from the "campielli" (squares) like... nipples on a flat-chested woman... or the top part of the stalk of an umbrella. "Nothing is a lie. It's words. It's not important." Best to do without similes in certain situations, Alice feels. Gulls slash open these sacks and pigeons attend the feast. Walking around Venice one can see many places that were frequently visited by Hemingway. Caffè Florian in San Marco, for example. Alain is waiting for her there. The place is buzzing. He has his favourite corner table and he has saved a chair for her. She sinks down. He calls over the waiter. Alain presents her with a red rose. "Since we are in Venice we must drink! Would you care for a Vanderbilt, a Vanderbilt Cornelius, a Vermouth, a Vermouth Cooler or a Vermouth No. 2?" "I don't think so." "Then how about a glass of Dom Bernardo Vincelli? No? Then perhaps, a Vin Chaud, a Vinho Verde, a Violet Fizz, a Virgin, a Vodka, a Vodka and bitter lemon, a Vodka and tonic, a Vodka Buck, a Vodka-Champagne punch, a Vodka Cobbler, a Vodka Collins, a Vodka Gibson, a Vodka Gimlet, a Vodka Grasshopper, a Vodka Gypsy, a Vodka Martini, a Vodka Orange Punch, a Vodka Sling, a Vodka Sour, or a Volga Boatman?" "What's a Volga Boatman?" "A Volga Boatman is an ounce and a half of vodka combined with the same amount of cherry brandy, an ounce and a half of orange juice and three – in some circumstances four – ice cubes. They are placed in a mixing glass and vigorously stirred. After that they are strained into a cocktail glass." "In that case I think I'd prefer a bottle of lager. Do you know if they have Stella Artois?" The waiter returns with a tall impressive glass filled with a fluid which resembles aerated urine. "Hemingway and Venice is love story," twinkly Alain chuckles. "But not conventional so." He wags a delicately manicured forefinger. Top drug dealers always patronise practitioners of a Shanghai pedicure. "It involve a deep falling in love with life that has in itself game, folly and, namely, big of all, *love*. Careless in its fizz, mad in its fire and instaneity, and all-inflammable in its ejaculations. But, perhaps, deep down, isn't this the precise Venetian magic? Isn't this the story of everyone who experience this place for first time? Is like first sex, no?" But when Alice reaches the Caffè Florian it is closed. The paint is peeling. It looks shabby and seedy. Hemingway isn't there. Neither is Alain. Alice walks back alone to the Hotel dei Dragomanni, where Alain is waiting for her in Room 12.

# 6

No, he is not really a drug dealer. That was just a story. He feels that only now can he tell her the truth. Now that he feels he knows her better. Alain confides he has never met a woman quite like Alice before. So fresh, so honest, so *charmante*. "I am tired in my soul and you make me... happy." He says he knows she would never betray him. The fact is... He hesitates again. "Let us go for a drink." They find a quiet bar beside a small canal. "Human beings are so insecure." He laughs. Their cocktails combine a dry white wine with crème de cassis. Ice cubes. A twist of lemon peel. The lights of the bar shine in the still water below. "Solace. Comfort. All love and friendship is based on that in the end." Alain says this as if he means it. He is suddenly so serious, so profound. "This is ours for the moment, but no more." From his pocket he produces a small dark book. "This was published in 1929," he explains. He hands it to her. *The Phenomenology of the Crisis*. "Do not open it. It contains secrets." "I won't." "She won't talk to you, you know," he adds. But did he really say those words? Pleasure comes from the brain, she thinks. "Thin fancies," she whispers. Alice reaches for the envelope in her pocket, then decides against withdrawing it. "You've got to keep me from going nuts." There – she's said it. Alain looks at her a little more directly. "You ought to relax too," he says. He finishes his drink and calls the waiter over for more. "Shall we dine tomorrow at the Gritti?" She leans forwards. Her face is now very close to his. "I feel depleted. On a plateau. To tell the truth..." Alain nods. He glances at the name of the bar. Alice can feel him committing the name and the street to memory. She has no time for such things. Venice is a city of numbers, electrical wires, windows and doors with thick protective bars. "I do not understand the subterranean channels of this dream." She wonders if she has really said those words. Pray for rain. It wipes away the stains. "Would you be afraid, with me?" The wind musses her hair. "I thought – let me put my body by his and wait for death." "In the magazine *Corona*, in 1930 –" She can make out, over there, the beginnings of a staircase. It rises into the darkness and dissolves. If she put all this together, with her photographs, perhaps with citations, what would be said? A name would be invoked. That of a sly melancholy meretricious grave careless hustler named Winifried. Alice gets rid of her cigarette stub in the marble ashtray. She looks at the bleak unhappy face of the man sitting opposite her. He's a great guy, she thinks. He understands when a woman is inside the dialectic. In a sort of natural dialectic... To cross a bedroom in darkness is not so difficult. Alain turns his head to one side. It is as if he is staring at something outside her field of vision.

# 7

Alice has little difficulty in locating the Europa Hotel where Donald Sutherland and Julie Christie stay. An invented name. *Click!* Alice presses her nose against the glass door. No, of course she doesn't. But she stands very close to it and peers in. What in the film is a reception area is now filled with chairs and tables, set out for dining. She observes the marble walls. Alice moves away. She is about to walk on. But there is a surprise on the wall to her left. *Click!*

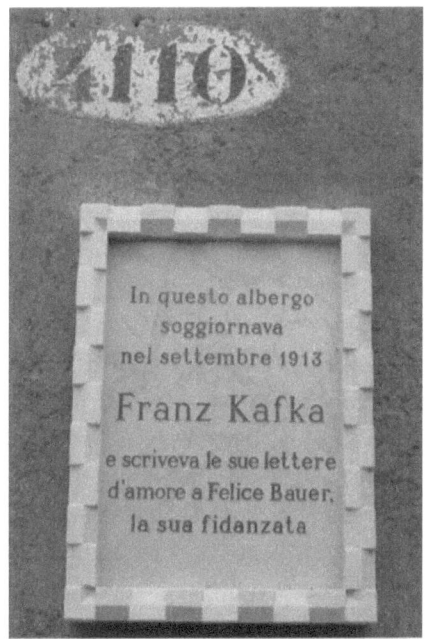

# 8

Alice puts "Kafka Venice" into a search engine. *Let's see what it ejaculates.* Venice uses Kafka Connect in the default pipeline to connect to a PostgreSQL database. A user can sink any topic on Kafka to a new table in Postgre via the Venice CLI. The table will be updated as new events arrive in Kafka. Users can then perform ad-hoc queries on this database and know that the results will be in sync with the rest of their pipeline. Confluent Hub hosts hundreds of... Kafka Connect works as the source-of-truth data storage inside Venice, and every data message will flow through Kafka to be persisted in the Venice data flow in platform. Kafka Mirror-Maker (Kafka MM) For... At its core, Venice is a sharded multi-tenant clustering software that leverages Kafka and RocksDB to power high throughput lookups for LinkedIn features (like People You May Know). You can learn... Is the Kafka Sink that ingest the data directly into Neo4j. How it works. It works in several ways. By providing a Cypher template. By ingesting the events emitted from another Neo4j instance via the Change Data Capture module. By providing a pattern extraction to a JSON or AVRO file. By managing a CUD file format. Cypher Template. It works with template Cypher queries stored into properties ... Is "Death in Venice" by Thomas Mann worth the read? Answer (1 of 2). What is your idea of a "good read"? This is a difficult question to answer. (2) Thomas Mann is one of the great German writers of the Twentieth Century. His literary career... HOTEL WITH

VIEW ON THE LAGOON. The palazzo is arranged with historical Venetian furniture. Throughout the interior you will see beautiful hand-made Murano glass chandeliers blown by the artist Archimede Seguso. Ancient marble decorates the walls, reception hall and the bar. Venetian cuisine is served in our restaurant on the waterfront terrace or in the relaxing romantic courtyard. A little jewel is the enchanting garden, an ideal place for a rest after a day in Venice. In the year 1913 Franz Kafka wrote a love letter from this hotel to his fiancée Felice Bauer. *We are proud to show Kafka's hand written worlds on hotel letter paper.* Alice smiles. They mean words. But perhaps the error is better. *Ancient marble decorates the walls, reception hall and the bar...* Yes. See the ancient marble surfaces as Donald Sutherland and Julie Christie enter and exit the hotel. Felice, Felice. Vexatious Felice. Her last letter is not an answer to his last letter. It is not in accordance with their agreement. So be it. Here, in Venice, unable to move. So many obstacles. And here alone. Talking to almost no one. Only the hotel staff. Take hold of the free hotel notepaper. Let your pen flow. Overflowing with unhappiness. A state of misery to be borne until the end of days. From his bed Kafka gazes at the clear Venetian sky. What is to be done? We shall have to part, Felice.

# 9

The church of San Nicolò dei Mendicoli is quite easy to find. You go inside. In the film it is bare and filled with scaffolding and builders' clutter. Now it is just another church, sumptuous with dreary ecclesiastical dross. Gilded. Baroque. It brings out the Protestant in her. The liking for what is bare, austere, straightforward. Protestantism watches its weight whereas Catholicism gluts itself on gold and does not care about its waist. Its waste. Its shining wastes. Its gross cherubs and dull-eyed Madonnas. Odd, how we have to thank that grotesque libidinous syphilitic brute Henry VIII for liberating England from this kitsch. Photography is not permitted. NO PHOTOGRAPHY. A sign showing the silhouette of a camera, with a diagonal line slashing it. And look, up there. That's where the slow-mo plank crashes into the high precarious cradle where Sutherland is comparing the mosaic tiles. You look around. No one is watching. The light is poor and you dare not use flash. Don't look – *now*.

*Click!*

# 10

Outside, you can see where Julie Christie stands, watching. Bored. You can see where the two weird sisters stand. Where they disappear from view. You follow their trail. Just round the corner you come to the latticed side-door where Christie catches up with them.

# 11

During her wanderings – her zigzag meanderings – Alice comes across a memorial to IL GRANDE COMPOSIT-ORE RUSSO PETRE IL'IĈ ĈAJKOVSKIJ and a wall bearing the inscription QVI ABITO LORD BYRON. Yes, so many cultural celebrities have passed through this city. Pietro Aretino. Milton. Erica Jong. Henry James. Patricia Highsmith. But Alice is chasing other ghosts. Clelia Matania. Hilary Mason. Massimo Serato. Adelina Poerio. And in chasing ghosts she wonders if she is creating her own... as a creation. With a fictional lover. Voiceover. Unreal city... city of mists. "Take off your hat." "Think big." "In a handwriting I could recognise." "What is it that you don't you feel quite clear about?" "Print my letters carefully, on good parchment." "Boundlessly inquisitive. Utterly forgetful." Streams of strangers flow by, paying you no attention. The people in the square resemble extras in a film. The paragraph falls silent. Your mind splashes out like the Rorschach test. She feels somewhat calmer, now. The graceful memory of old suffering. "Bordering on nihilism." "It may equal D or Q." It is not worth making a point of their last night together because it will only be the beginning of another story, the story of their parting. "Rien ne va plus." "Oh dear." Alice becomes aware of a great fatigue. Everything has been written. The early darkness is beginning. She returns to the hotel tired out, with her mind blank. In the mirror her mouth looks grim, almost cruel. On the exposed sheet of the bed a series of fresh paragraphs can be seen, announcing certain modifications of style. Alice smiles. No matter. She is organised now. But doubts persist. She could do with a Golden Screw. Where in hell is Alain? He promised to be here. In the end, in Venice, everyone is just passing through. Everyone here is a goddam tourist.

# 12

"Dempsey says –" "That's why they shot it." Alain is neither a specialist bookseller satisfying excessively affluent customers who seek exceptionally rare and unimaginably filthy erotica, nor is he a drug dealer to the elite. *Pas du tout.* After their second night together, at breakfast, he whispers the truth. He is a top assassin. There is a highly secretive organisation based in Venice which hires paid killers to eliminate the antagonists of the super rich and certain governments. He is one of those professionals. Alice listens, enthralled. She fondles his hand. Her head swims. She applies pressure with her foot. Now at last is the moment, yes. She understood. She opened her arms and smiled. It is only later, when *The Matrix Resurrections* comes out, that she looks up Keanu Reeves and learns about his John Wick franchise. Alain tells her that he operates according to the highest standards. Each year he assassinates just one individual, to order. He gets a down-payment of a quarter of a million dollars and the remaining three quarters upon completion of the task. Paid into a Swiss bank, naturally. "And if you fail in your mission?" Alain smiles a cold mirthless smile. "I have never failed... But if I did then I in turn would become..." He pauses, as the script requires. He produces his best dryly ironic voice: "A target in turn." He tells her a little more. The target is supplied to him on the first day of January, via an encrypted email. He then has the rest of the year to accomplish his task. Naturally it is unwise to leave it to

New Year's Eve (although he did, once). "Gosh," Alice says, biting into her almond croissant. "I tell you this because I trust you." He holds her left wrist. "Tell no one." "Golly, I won't," she promises. Although in fact she did. Back in England she told her best friends Suzy, Janine and Brenda. They each one assured her that Alain was a top grade bullshitter, and she should never have fallen for his spiel. She winks. She giggles. Girl talk. Her lizard tongue drags shining saliva across her upper lip. "It wasn't his spiel I fell for."

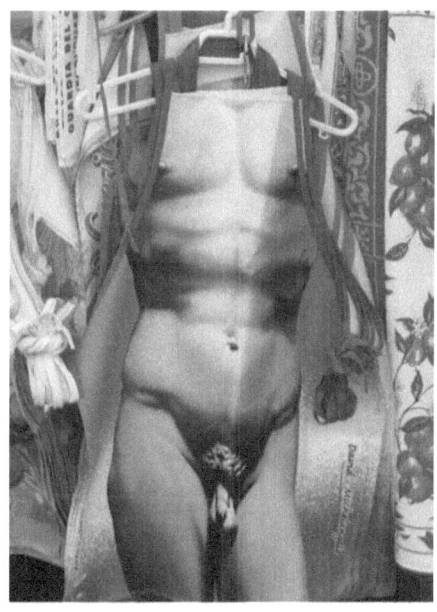

# 13

"I opened the front door, leaving the key in the lock." Alain is telling her another of his assassin's tales. He insists they are true. He assures her that he only liquidates those who deserve liquidation. Plump paedophiles, pink pusillanimous politicians, pox-ridden princes, pungent ponces, plangent procrastinators... The exterminator. Ridding the world of bugs, pests and vermin. Lice, rats, cockroaches... "I opened the front door, leaving the key in the lock. I put my right hand into my pocket. I rolled a cartridge in my fingers." On the wall there was a portrait of Guillaume Apollinaire. "And then?" "I slammed him on the nose with everything I had." "Crikey!" "I looked down at him. He was a bloody pulp. 'Convalescing?' I said with a sneer." The day had long since broken. The Italian square. The purity of a dream. The disquieting muses. Mystery of a hotel room. The anxious journey. Autumn melancholy. The enigma of fate. There were fragments everywhere. Some are still here. They are luminous, with a tendency to wriggle. Yes. See! Pinkish-grey lizards chase each other in short, quick runs. "I bought glucose tablets and some smoked ham." He squeezed, very softly. The vicious crack of the shot boomed across the square. In those days he used a .308 calibre rifle. Alice looks out of the window of the bar, on to the waters of the Grand Canal. "Make it a very dry Martini," Alain says. "A double." "And I'll have a Bermuda Highball," says Alice. She adds: "It's what you say. An odd coincidence." "I, too, have had dreams, terrible dreams." Duplication, inversion, fission, repetition. "The blueness of a garment, the breath of a lip, the voice of a bird. The objects in the room. A mask. Flowers. Fruit." They depart and end up in that monumental corridor where she takes her last steps backward. A few scattered notes gradually acquire volume. Alice begins to cry. "I *am* real!"

# 14

"Standing on solid ground when –" Delirium! "No, she didn't. She didn't say anything." "*The Blue Spill*. Is very rare, very disgusting." "A book?" "Yes, a book. Only five copy exist." It was not a typo. Alain sometimes struggles with his plurals. If he is an assassin it seems odd that he does not know that the word "death" appears seven times at line endings in *Pericles*. Nor is he as well travelled as he pretends. He does not know Jonesport, Maine, at all. He has never even seen a hummingbird, its throat glittering like a ruby. Was Alain flesh and blood? Did he have a working pulse? Clamour of music, hurrying feet, city of echoing alleyways. *Oh quante sono incantatrici, oh quanti incantator tra noi, che non si sanno!* In Venice the sharp silver sunlight gradually effaces the stigmata of kisses. The city invites the grand style. Have you heard of Herr von N's adventures there? *Give me fresh garments and a cocktail shaker*. Ho, there! Alice is mad again! She is not in Venice at all, she is in a lunatic asylum. Joker! And now the seams need caulking. "I said I don't know." Have the flying job-boom cleared and lashed to the monkey-rail. A storm is on its way. "I'm going now."

# 15

Across the canal to the side where Olga Rudge lived. She was with Pound to the end. And later, buried alongside. Theatrical youthful bombastic Ezra! He'd come a long way from those younger days, that London daze. That café in New Oxford Street where you could look up and see yourself staring from the bed of a clear lagoon. His heart-of-gold intertwined with *fleurs de lys* and star-spangled oddities. Brave pioneering sailor of the China Seas! Cowboy songster with fierce blue eyes! And later, in Paris, he boxed with Hemingway, who in those days was tall, handsome, serene. So W said. Perhaps not much cop, Ezra, as a boxer – but now a great poet and a great impresario. But with gold there was debt, with debt there was usury. No picture is made to endure nor to live with but is made to sell and to sell quickly. Litfic in a nutshell! A murrain. It blunts the needle. It rusts the craft. On the first floor that room with a mirrored ceiling. W saw him once, no more, at all events, beneath that ceiling of glass. The circulations of genius. Big fish in a little lagoon. The years pass. He shrank in old age, Pound. He shouldered a bearded weariness. As Joyce progressed from tidy narrative to verbal phantasmagoria, so the *Cantos*. M'amour, m'amour. What do I love and where are you? To hell with the Tombs Slithery Souplement! Alain held her as close as he could and tried to think about nothing. "Phone call from Brazil." Alain lies back with his head on her stomach. They can hear the sound of glass breaking somewhere out there in the night. Alice remembers Ottawa under snow. What Ezra Pound said about the luminous detail. It shiningly summons up – evokes – produces – a dimension which is implied by that specific aspect. The *Cantos* are to be lived with over many years. Like a spouse. Each new reading – a reading of many pages at a time – is – is – is a new bewilderment. So it should be, for so it was meant to be. So Donald – *Donald!* – told her. Ezra Pound wanted to break the pentameter. To smash the expectations which blank verse had blankly pressed down upon the bedazzled generations. Writers, Alain says, wryly. He gets a shoulder holster out of the drawer and straps it on. Next he slips a Colt .38 automatic into it. Outside the corridor was still. "Tell no one I have been to Berlin." "I won't." "Eat. It will make you less sad." Her heart was clenched as if by an iron hand. No trace of twilight remained in the sky. When he comes back, she's there. In bed. "I told you they don't understand." "Does it hurt?" "No. I'll be fine." He rinses his hands under the cold tap. He is wearing his soft ripple rubber climbing boots. "The only right thing to do is to come to terms with circumstances as they are." The man had fallen forward, his right arm outstretched. Alain laughs. It is a rather ghoulish laugh. "I'll be all right in the morning." Alice reads to the foot of the page.

# 16

It is so long since she saw the film its sequencing is no longer clear in her mind. She has to watch it again on her laptop while Alain is out, to get the order right. The Hertfordshire opening. Julie Christie's silent scream. The abrupt cut to a drill piercing a wall overlooking the Grand Canal. This is the terrace of the Bauer Hotel. On the far side of the Grand Canal can be seen Santa Maria della Salute. And then the scene in the restaurant, the encounter with the two sisters, the fainting scene, the hospital, and then the departure by launch. The watery journey encounters an obstacle. A crime scene. It is the aftermath of a murder. The Venice serial killer has struck again! The police are dusting for fingerprints on the handrail of a bridge. Some of them stand on a balcony overlooking the canal. Among them is Inspector Longhi. *Renato Scarpa*. And look, it is still here, just as in the film. The bridge, the balcony, the building – Palazzo Tetta – where the canal splits into two. Half a century passes. Venice outlives its ghosts. Alice is in a melancholy mood this morning. It is partly the season, the weather. Partly it comes from looking up the cast to see what happened to them in later years. Julie Christie, born 14 April 1940, is currently still alive. Donald Sutherland, born 17 July 1935, is currently still alive. Giorgio Trestini, born 26 March 1937, seems to be still alive. Presumably the child actress Sharon Williams is also still alive. But her child co-star Nicholas Salter is not. He died long ago, in Brixton prison. Apparently a troubled young man. He hanged himself. Further details are unavailable. Murkiest of all is the fate of Adelina Poerio, the dwarf. In one version she was a celebrity dwarf, a beautiful woman who'd dumped her husband and run off with a normal-size lover. She sat on the lover's lap while he applied makeup for her final scene. But in another version she was the deformed child of a very rich family which cast her out. She was found working at a car wash in Rome. She was just what the film-makers were looking for. A hideous-looking dwarf. In this version she had difficulty walking and there was no make-up in that final scene. Further details are unavailable. Adelina Poerio must surely by now be dead. Alice has a vague notion that the life span of dwarfs is shorter (no joke – no way) than that of ordinary people. Others in that luminous cast have unequivocally gone into the dark. Clelia Matania died on 14 October 1981, aged 63. Massimo Serato died on 22 December 1989, aged 73. Leopoldo Trieste died on 25 January 2003, aged 85. Hilary Mason died on 5 September 2006, aged 89. David Tree died on 4 November 2009, aged 94. Bruno Cattaneo died on 8 May 2019, aged 80. Ann Rye died on 27 August 2019, aged 84. Renato Scarpa died on 30 December 2021, aged 82.

# 17

"Where have you been?" "To Dorsoduro." "Dealing?" "No, of course not." "Women are unusually intuitive." "Remember what the man said. A liar is as beautiful as apple trees when they are in blossom." "He was lying." "It makes you wonder what people do at 5.30 in the afternoon." "Fetch me nourishment. I fancy a Gimlet. Shaken, not stirred." "I thought I had made myself clear. Remember what the man said. Really, it's not me who is writing this crazy book. It's you and the receptionist. It's the waiter, the sculptor, the seller of cigarettes. It's that couple crossing the square and that man at the bar and those two girls at the table in the corner. It's that group of middle-aged French tourists at the next table, where the waiter is leaning across, proffering a giant pepper pot." "There is no next table. There are no French tourists. There is no giant pepper pot." Alain smiles. Such a gentle delicate half-melancholy smile. "Look! A knot!" "Eisenstein's editing aims at certainty." "Oh, do let me help to undo it!" "We can't go on like this." "As a matter of fact: we can. And we will."

# 18

There is so little time to prepare. At the railway station they are selling English language guides to Venice and Italian translations of *Animal Farm* and *Fifty Shades of Grey*. Alice has only read the second of those immortal classics. The guide supplies useful phrases. *Mi sono perso. Non capisco. Quanto costa? Qual è la password Wi-Fi? Il Wi-Fi è gratis?* That's all the Italian a girl needs in this city. Besides, Alain is fluent in Italian. He gabbles at waiters and they gabble back. *Venice in a Day*. Alice looks at what has to be crammed in. The fish market. Eh? She has not come all this way to buy fresh fish. Nor does their hotel room have a cooker. No chance of a quick tasty fry-up with some yummy beef-fat-marinated oven chips. The Rialto Bridge. About as much fun as a check-out in Sainsbury's on a Saturday morning. Crossing it with her, Alain stops to buy two cheap Made-in-China plastic masks. For bedroom fun, later. Role-play. To be not who they are, really. Really? It makes her think of that movie with Hugh Grant in, the Polanski one. And then on to Piazzo San Marco. It's full of Chinese tourists. Mobs led by tour guides with flags on slender wire poles strapped to a backpack. Hordes with selfie sticks. Alice wants to get away from Piazzo San Marco as quickly as possible. She has no desire to linger. Try a traditional aperitif at the Caffè Quadro? Who in fuck wants to be booze-fuddled at 11am? A glass of Prosecco at the Caffè Florian? Ditto. Besides, she loathes Prosecco. A nasty thin fizzy sweet vastly overrated wine. If she has to swill down a flute she'd rather it was Cava. Or better still, a frosted goblet of Taittinger. Not that she's wild for fizz. She's more of a lamb and fine red wine kind of gal. Next stop is the Basilica San Marco. To maximise your time make sure to reserve tickets in advance. Once the private chapel of the doge. An odd word, doge. Allow ten minutes. Afterwards admire the Campanile. When doing Venice In A Day there is not sufficient time for the Palazzo Ducale, so cross the square and turn left at the two columns topped by the former and current patron saints of Venice. On your left watch out for the famous restored Ponte dei Sospiri – the Bridge of Sighs. After crossing the Ponte del Vin you will soon find yourself in the Castello district, a good place to experience everyday Venetian life. But Alice would rather not – not this variety. She is indifferent to the city's strong history of craftsmanship. She has no wish whatever to visit the gondola workshops or the manufacturers of papier-mâché masks or the glass-blowers. She is equally indifferent to the city's art. Not for her the Accademia and its ginger-haired angels or the kitsch on display at the Guggenheim. Dreary daubs by frauds like Cy Twombly and Rothko are not for Alice. She has little stomach for art anchored to explanatory prose. George Frederick Watts down in Guildford – she liked that gallery. *I paint ideas, not things.* And Tenniel – now *there* was an artist. But you won't find him in this Italian Disneyland. Step this way folks for masterpieces by Bellini, Titian, and Tintoretto? Blessed relief: CHISUO PER FERIE. On she goes, Alice. Zigzag, zigzag. She has planned her route in advance. You need to, in this labyrinth. It takes a while to realise that the name plates on the walls are different to what is marked on the Michelin map. It is like finding yourself on Regent Street only to discover that the sign reads Street of Crocodiles. And now – clever Alice! – she reaches the place where fate led John Baxter. The Palazzo Grimani. And it is just as it is in the film. The little bridge. The water gate, which Donald Sutherland locks behind him. That gate where Julie Christie clings to the bars and cries, "Darlings!" Laura Baxter knows her husband and her daughter will be reunited in death. It was derelict when Roeg filmed there and stayed that way for the rest of the century. Then it was renovated. Today it is an art gallery. Alice goes inside.

# 19

Standard kitsch. Three electroplated wheelchairs. An elongated Vespa. A carpet of tiny skulls. If you take your shoes off you may walk the length of them in your socks. No thanks. Some photographs of nude women, devoid of sensuality. A room with a blue glowing wall and raggedy drapes. The usual banal orthodoxies passing themselves off as innovative contemporary art. In their own way the equivalent of those gleaming acclaimed dead modern novels on the table in Waterstones. Gripping, brilliantly inventive, extraordinarily moving, dazzling, powerfully humane, provocative, remarkable, timely, fabulous, dazzling, quite brilliant, pulling you into the lives of the characters in the most absorbing way. Tablets to be swallowed by those with easy incurious sensibilities. For readers who would frown at the word *sensibilities*. Alice moves towards the window. *Oh. My. God.* This is fucking unbelievable! If this was in a novel you wouldn't fucking believe it!

# 20

Daphne du Maurier wrote "Don't Look Now" when she was 63. It was the last short story she ever wrote. It is a tale of a marriage under stress; of a wife fending off a crack-up; of the weight of the past. Of mortality, decay, memory. And death. A fiction, conventional in form, quiet in language, which seethes beneath its placid surface with unarticulated intense desperate anxieties. Daphne du Maurier died in her sleep on 19 April 1989, of bronchopneumonia. By then she was skeletal in appearance and weighed only six stones. She was inspired by seeing a child in Venice. And then she saw the child's face. It was not a child at all but an adult dwarf. *It was not a child at all but a little thick-set woman dwarf, about three feet high, with a great square adult head too big for her body...* And as Alice stands at the window of the Palazzo Grimani a female dwarf comes out of the alleyway opposite. She has sunglasses, pushed up across her hair. She is moving towards a motor boat, anchored below, covered by a red sheet. The dwarf is laughing and chatting on her phone. Alice starts taking a sequence of pictures. *Click, click, click, click, click!* She tracks the dwarf, who turns right and crosses the Ponte Novo and then vanishes from sight. Ten, nine, eight, seven, six, five, four, three, two, one. *Coming to get you!*

# 21

If there is death in Venice, Alice doesn't see it. A serial killer is not out there, despatching locals and visitors. There is no plague, no typhoid outbreak. She sees no rats – white or black. The 2020 pandemic is still in the future – and when it hits she'll be in Brooklyn. Later, when she looks up novels set in Venice, she sees that there are an astonishing number of them. Many of them seem to be crime novels. It is as if for novelists Venice is not enough. It has to be pumped full of imaginary slaughter and extreme emotion. As if everyday life is not adequate. As if this city's ghosts were insufficient. Alice walks on until she reaches the little bridge by Santa Maria dei Miracoli. Donald Sutherland walked here. It's after he witnesses the corpse fished from the canal basin by the little bridge on Corte Maggiore. He leaves the Bishop and next thing he's here, on an eccentric route back to his hotel. Roeg assumes his audience will not know Venice. His geography is that of a dream. Sutherland walks over the bridge, going in the wrong direction. A quick shot, no more than that. Behind the actor we see the church of Santa Maria dei Miracoli. Pound's church. Pietro Lombardo carved the mermaids. Alice pays the woman in the kiosk and walks to the front. Alice sits and stares. She is underwhelmed. Later she tells Alain nothing of this. "I didn't go to Marienbad. I may go soon. I shall stay for three weeks. I shall lead a quiet life, the way I like it." Now dusk is approaching. Alain's voice – the way he speaks. So dense and yet so airy. "What's going on?"

"Everything is permitted." "What is your greatest ambition?" "The Bernstein Straße (B 49)." "Will you write about us?" "I ought to live here. It's a good town to walk in." They sit at a table and finger their glasses. Now they are both smoking cigarettes again. Alain is not visible, or else he is very blurred, to one side. Her voice rises a couple of notches. "Are you leaving Venice at once?" "No, not today." He looks at her for a long time without expression. "What role does the camera play? Who in fact speaks in a book?" There is nothing to see, except peeling paint. "Nothing is true." Alice goes to switch off the light. "I wouldn't be surprised," Alain says. "Across the Danube." He is completely in command of himself. In the angle of the wall is a motionless spider. Alain asks her if she's listening. Alice shakes her head. He sees the white scar just below her chin. "It's over," she says.

# 22

On the flight back, when this is all over, Alice glances out of the window. Englishtown, New Jersey, is still so far away. She observes an unidentifiable land mass protruding through the cloud layer. It resembles islands in a misty sea. Alice reaches for her little Canon and takes one last picture. *Click!* The steward, who is dressed entirely in white paper, leans forwards and whispers in her ear. "Never mind what they say. Buy a return ticket every time." "Is it urgent?" "Yes. Something has happened." Alice waits calmly for the dialogue to continue. She asks for a gin and tonic and drinks it with her favourite medication. As she closes her eyes she thinks of Roeg's later movies. After *Don't Look Now* he worked again with Donald Sutherland, casting him as Axel Heyst in *Victory*. Filmed in sultry Thailand it remains the finest cinematic adaptation of any Joseph Conrad novel. Or might have been. Because the project fell through. Not to worry. Roeg's next film, *Deadly Honeymoon*, was, famously, another classic. Or might have been. Roeg began filming W. D. Richter's script of the Lawrence Block crime thriller *Deadly Honeymoon*. But five days into the shoot in Louisiana MGM terminated Roeg's contract and replaced him with Elliot Silverstein. Not to worry. These misfortunes resulted in Roeg making his most accessible classic – *Out of Africa*. But, no – that project went nowhere. It joined the library of imaginary films, beside the great hall of novels which were never written, and the lives and loves which split in two and went one way instead of another. This way, folks, for the Museum of Extinguished Possibilities. Alice has another G & T. Her mind turns cloudy. She clamps her noise-cancelling headphones to her head. She selects her favourite option and closes her eyes.

# 23

Julie Christie encounters the two weird sisters outside San Nicolò dei Mendicoli. Donald Sutherland is wrestling with the gargoyle. John Baxter watches anxiously as his wife wanders off and disappears from view, going the same way as that pair of troubling, sinister women. Cinematic magic! Bewildering geography. Venetian wonderment. Yes, Laura Baxter is now walking in the Giardini Pubblici, a long way from that Venice-in-Peril church. The three women walk past a decayed, anorexic statue of Envy. Another stony observer. Since Nic Roeg was here the statue has lost major limbs. It's a disturbing piece. Alice is slightly uncertain of its gender. The breasts, sagging down towards those protuberant ribs, are almost female, though the contorted square-jawed face seems to be a man's. The genitals are hidden behind a lump of stone.

# 24

"I make no promises." As Alice walks back to San Marco she stumbles upon another *Don't Look Now* location. Christie and Sutherland walk across a square with an arch in the background. Supposedly – can you trust the internet? – Viale Trento. Supposedly – a website asserts – the Largo Marinai d'Italia. The couple are bickering. Laura wants John's permission to meet the weird sisters again. "It's ridiculous." "To get rid of the emptiness." The camera pans to the gate at Rio Tera San Isepo. The residence just to the left of it is painted red. Was this done for the film, Alice wonders. Antonioni did exactly that for *Blow-Up*. Or was it simply serendipity? John and Laura pass through and pause just the other side. A metaphor. The argument continues. "Thanks for the memories." And then, in exasperation: "Go on, go on..." John walks away across Campo San Isepo. Alice does not follow him. Instead she returns through the gateway. She notices that on the walls either side of the gate are posters advertising a mosaic display: IL SERRAGLIO DELLE MERAVIGLIE. And that house even today, all these decades later, still has a dull reddish pallor.

# 25

Alain has never seen *Don't Look Now*. He prefers action movies. Bond, Bourne, superheroes. "Is because I work alone. Is because I am reliable and cautious. Is why I am undetected. Is why my secrets are intact. I steal but no one notices." "Does a flame feel pain?" "It is all written down." "Maybe I should start taking my pills again." "Hung out to dry." "Jewel thieves or murderers?" Alice feels a curious sensation. A tingling paralysis. She decides to remain where she is. She nods. "It's part of my job to remember conversations. I can lip-read too." Alain's face is empty. The clock on the wall has stopped. It makes Alice think of the cover of her old Penguin edition of *The Trial*.

# 26

Alice finds quite easily the bridge and the covered echoing walkway where John Baxter leads blind Heather back to her hotel. It is close to the opera house and not very far from the Calle Dose da Ponte.

# 27

As she stands on this bridge and looks down into the water Alice is amazed to see a shoal of fish swim by. Dream creatures. They flit across the grey flow of her mind. November's mists give birth to inaccurately transmitted words. This city's symmetries have a finality as sharp and straight as regret itself. O water, water of love... Hyperbolic pangs. "Is this being recorded?" "Every word."

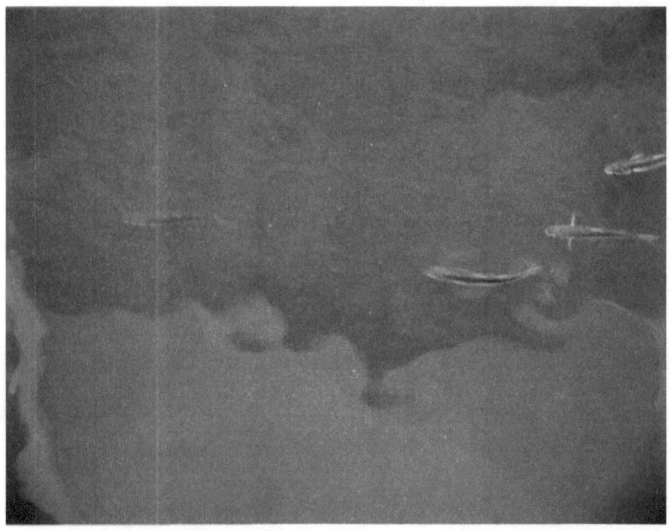

# 28

*La nostalgia del poeta...* That year of war. To disrupt our normal senses of scale, space, and the relationships between things. To create a sense of dream. The plaster bust, the mannequin, the fish mould, the obelisk. Compressed into a narrow format. To create a claustrophobic and enigmatic space. The forms bear no apparent relation to each other. A combination of displaced objects and elusive meaning. Giorgio di Chirico (1888-1978). He lived as long as Nicolas Roeg.

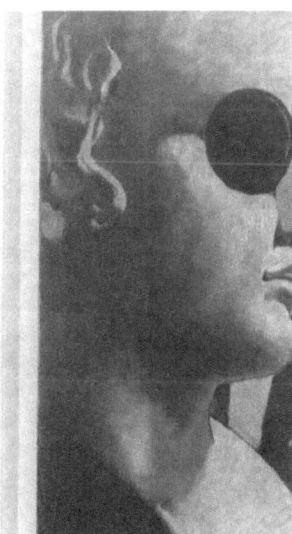

# 29

The steps where Donald Sutherland notices the waterlogged doll. "Etre un vieillard, fini, à vingt-trois..." Alain sighs. Over their heads is a commemorative inscription. He tells Alice the story. "A young man is in love with a girl. But she does not return his love. For years. And then. And after that... They have other love affairs. But neither marries." He pauses, lights a cigarette. "Suicide and murder are the sort of things I mean," she says. She adds: "It's an extraordinary coincidence, isn't it?" Alain shakes his head and then the pepper pot. "The situation was very reminiscent of a story in Guiseppe Raimondi's *Notizie dall' Emilia.*"

# 30

It is about here, Alice realises, that John Baxter sees his own funeral barge from the vaporetto. "Laura!" And then: "Laura!" When the vessel docks he runs in the wrong direction, in order to pass Harry's bar. In the background can be glimpsed the Bauer Hotel and the windows of the room where the famous sex scene was filmed.

# 31

"The presentation of the facts," Alice says, "is made in terms of textual references, signatures upon documents, their dates, and the idiom in which the documents were written. From this standpoint the Cantos are the long poem of a wandering scholar without chair, without portfolio." "The study of slang," says Alain, "especially the secret language of thieves or gypsies, seems to have started in 1549. That was the year of the anonymous publication in Venice of *Il modo novo da intender la lingua zerga cioè parlar furbesco*." "Mind the volcano!" "Who is he?" "The thanatologist wishes to know why and how it was used." "The operator will connect you." "I doubt it." The words are cut short as Alice pushes through the swing doors and into the street.

# 32

Look! There is the canal basin where the bishop asks the cop on the boat what's happening. "I hope it's not another murder." "We should go." So it is. Each morning Alice visits a new location, sometimes more than one. Alain, meanwhile, disappears on important business. They meet up whenever suits them. Lunchtimes sometimes. Late afternoon. Harry's Bar at six. The mist never goes. She sits gestureless and mute. "You can put away your Penguin Freud. Put away your crystal ball." "I asked you to go. Why haven't you gone?" "Because I stayed." "I know. But you know..." "Well that's just it. I meant to tell you. I can't..." "For three months I read *À la Recherche du Temps Perdu* every day." "The architecture of the film." "Two, really. The first a movement, chiefly narrative, towards disillusion. The other, more intermittent, toward revelation. Rising to that point where lost time is found and fixed forever in art." And at the end we hear the bell. Resilient ferruginous interminable fresh and shrill. "It was never made." "A beam of light glimmering at the top of the house." "I see you're admiring my little box." "Let me in – quickly. Don't put any light on." "Ouvre ta robe." Alice notices a very black 313 on a very white door. *Give me fresh garments and a cocktail of drugs.*

# 33

"Have you seen it?" "Never about what they seem to be about at first." "My address." Alain lights up a Gitane. "Wrong place at the wrong time." "Did you know that Céline died on the same day as Hemingway?" "Not really." "Time zones. Americans are always later than the French." "There is nothing left over." "Bad timing." "Where was the gun hidden?" "His weakness lay in never having known either marriage or the accepted adventures of the heart." Alice nods. "Uh-huh." She remains seated, lost in thought. "With his love of sharp contrasts he opens his sequel on an indoor midwinter scene." "The eyes, the expression, I don't know." At first Alain doesn't answer. His eyes are blinded with the rain. "The white that surrounds the words." Alice uncrosses her legs. "I recognize what you're saying." "It's the only place worth –" "Exactly. Consider the feathers of a lobster..." "The echoes remain." "We have no control, we live on threads." A slow, serious voice. "If we want to know what the poem is about, we had better read it as it was written, in the shadow of many books." Her hand is tapping out a rhythm on the table. There is sadness in her words. "Tatters of lamentation. Tatters of degradation." A strange turn of events. The book slips from her lap. As it falls to the floor, a photograph drops out of it. "After his fourth novel... finished!" Holding her close, he burst into tears. There is a scratch on her wrist. She turns to the left and walks rapidly away. "I couldn't follow his logic. I think he was on acid or something." A jongleur was also a joglar. A bright reciter of texts. The permutations. Perhaps a tumbler. Always an actor. "What a performance!" Magician, sorcerer, trickster. Spinner of words. Uqbar, Orbis, Tertius... What's missing? Pivot points. Ho, there! Fetch voltage! Jolts! Sparks. Sparklers. Versa, reversals, magic mushrooms. They grew beside the great lake, if you knew where to look. Above the road, below an outcrop of pines. They grew close to the route of the abandoned railway. In the grass you sometimes saw an old sleeper. A scrap of the old track. Everything changes, Venice endures.

# 34

"It's about a man and a woman in Venice." Alain smiles. He is not afraid to be a half-way person. The restaurant is only a quarter full. It's too late to do anything now but go to bed. "Why did you do that?" "My despair, my symphony." "There must be more." "No. No, there's nothing more." "We were talking about the film last night." "Tell me why you came here." "I shall stop now. I can't go on any longer." Alain asks her the time. When she tells him he looks horrified. "So soon?" He pushes his chair back. "I must go." "I expected to be bored and resentful. Instead I twiddled the pages in eager gobbling of succeeding words." "Smart girl!" "It then becomes simple to understand the way in which the Cantos are put together." "How could I forget?"

# 35

*So.* This is the door leading into the sisters' second pension. Donald Sutherland leads Hilary Mason back here, after escorting her from her police cell. This is the door Clelia Matania runs out of, trying to find Donald Sutherland after he's departed. This is the door Julie Christie rushes out of, hoping to catch up with him. *Find him!*

# 36

Julie Christie runs frantically into this space. She moves to the right, then swerves to the left. She runs off into the dark alleyway, in panicky pursuit.

# 37

Quatrefoils, ogives. Sapphire waters. Marble, gold. Moorish windows. Marcel Proust. Corinthian columns. Colour, diastasis. Those horses. Henry James. Frescoes, mosaics. Jasper embossed. Emerald paved. Golden angel. Thomas Mann. Gondola serenade. Dead-ends. City of.

# 38

"Injective." "Surjective." "The rest is dross." "You don't have to say you love me." "As for the rest, I have to make a report." "You're thinking about something. And that makes you forget to talk." "Pictures?" "Photos." Alice likes to read a set of proofs twice. Once for the defects and once for the virtues of the text. Alain lights his famous cigarillo. He was in a song once. "It looks as if disappointment must be inevitable." The years pass. Memory crumbles. Was Venice an easy place to film in? Not at all. The tides play havoc with the continuity. "I was determined not to show the tourist side, the side featured in endless travel documentaries, and deliberately kept out of St Mark's Square. You never see it." Well, yes and no. It's true the viewer never sees Piazza San Marco. But there is a shot of Piazzetta San Marco. After John says goodbye to Laura and she goes off on the vaporetto to catch a flight back to England, to see their son after his fire-drill accident, Donald Sutherland walks towards the Campanile. In the background you see the two granite columns of San Marco and San Teodoro. It is bad luck to walk between these columns. As John Baxter approaches the camera the columns enclose him like a trap. His fate is now inevitable. He will never see Laura again.

# 39

*Sex City.* Secret city. Shutters, blinds, bars, narrow passages. City of voyeurs, photographers, film-makers. Novella mongers, criminal plots. Look! Look now. No, of course Alain is not an assassin. Nor does he deal in crystal meth. He is what he was from the start, a dealer in rare erotica. He shows Alice his wares. A first edition of *A Treatise of the Use of Flogging In Venereal Affairs: ALSO of The Office of the LOINS and REINS* by John Henry Meibomius, M.D. (London, 1718). The 1786 edition of Knight's *Discourse on the Worship of Priapus.* Two graphic unpublished letters by Georges Bataille, together with a chapter, handwritten, excised from the published *Le Bleu du Ciel.* An unpublished erotic novella, in typescript, by Pauline Réage. The extraordinary and uninhibited memoirs of infamous Penelope Ashe. "In the last analysis, I wonder why I'm enjoying myself so much." "I've had dreams too, but mine died." "I can't bear all these painted wounds." "This hotel must be a century old." "Tonight we're extras. They are the main characters." "Where?" "Over there."

# 40

"William Shakespeare. Jane Austen. Joseph Conrad. William Faulkner. Malcolm Lowry. George Orwell. Jim Thompson. So many great writers never went to Venice. Not even once." "I'm in a hurry. Goodbye." "Alright. Where will you be?" "Those whom we have loved die twice." "I should like to have it explained." "It's extraordinary when you think about it. *L'Eden et après* released in 1970. *N. a pris les dés* in 1971. *Tout va bien* in 1972. And *Don't Look Now* in 1973." "The rejection of conventional tonality." "Quite." "A dodecaphinc system. Improvisation. A narrative shaped like life itself by chance. The intrusion of the random." "Collage. All that we have lost." "We?" "Oui."

# 41

"Watch your knuckles!" "Eh?" Pause. "Oh. I see. *Merci*."
"On a white horse." "Hi! Everything okay?" "You've done
enough." "The girl has beautiful dark eyes and a strange
way of looking." "Either drunk, drugged or insane." "The
sky is now dark." Alain departs in an ebullient mood. He
is off to a decayed palazzo to visit a depraved countess.
He is confident she will buy those extraordinary and
uninhibited memoirs. Alice goes off in search of the bar
where John Baxter waits while Laura attends the séance
with the two strange sisters. It's on the other side of the
Grand Canal. She finds it without too much difficulty.
First there's the alleyway that Julie Christie walks down,
at the end of which is the pension where the weird ones
are staying. The room they will later vacate. And at the
other end is the bar where Baxter drinks too much. But it
is no longer a bar. On this day it is Ristorante Pizzeria
Dolfin.

# 42

"The missed connections." "Give me a little time." "But there wasn't – I mean, I must just have dreamed –" "The look on someone's face. I hear you. But what are you saying?" "Fitfully, I imagine?" "It's first, second and third act, and it has to be in that order. And if you're not doing that, they're not buying it." "Look!" The mist. Disconnections. After the abortion you needed to get away. A few days on your own. To sort yourself out.

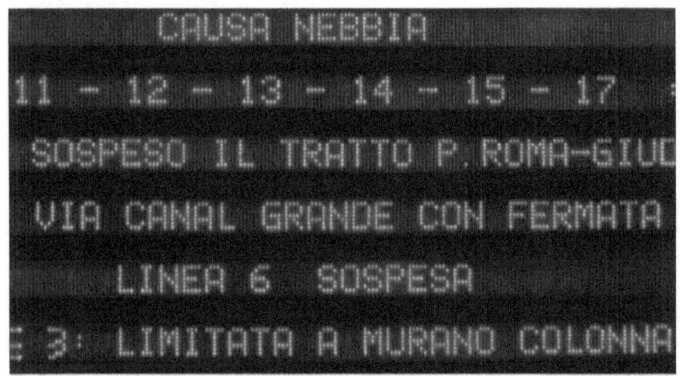

# 43

"It feels like I've woken up with a start from a confused sleep." The garden, like everything else, is empty. "Alain? I was besotted. He was a sculptor. He collected used materials and re-assembled them." On the wall there are three yellow posters, side by side. "You've been smoking something, haven't you?" "Let's get one thing straightened out." "Still think it was a set piece?" Alice sways and falls forward. "Combat the diegesis!" "I think I'll go and spray the apples. And you?" "I will find the sea again." "All the rest is just anecdote." "Those fingerprints." "Those gloves."

# 44

Nothing has happened yet. Alain looks tired, as if he has been on a long journey. Alice photographs the corridor down which the homicidal dwarf ran. The bust makes her think of the end of *2001: A Space Odyssey*. So does the scene where the sighted sister views their new room at Hotel La Fenice et des Artistes. The beds and the space and the simplicity of the room are reminiscent of the furnishings of the room at the end of Kubrick's film. The furniture of rebirth.

# 45

And at the end of Via Garibaldi you might almost be in Vienna... "Do you know where you're going?" "Straight on." "It's not always easy." Venice, Vienna, Vancouver. So many cities beginning with the letter V. "That's interesting." Orson Welles filmed in Vienna for six weeks at the end of 1948. Later he went to Venice to film *Othello*. Calle Larga Widmann. Ponte del Piovan o del Volto. Roeg pays homage. Micheál Mac Liammóir – now there was a character! And what a production. A fight starts in Morocco and finishes in Rome. The magic of cinema. In Hitchcock's *The Thirty-nine Steps* the scream of the cleaner discovering the body dissolves into the whistle of the train taking Robert Donat north to Scotland – a moment duplicated by Julie Christie's scream at seeing Donald Sutherland carrying the dead body of their daughter which cuts to the ferocious squeal of a drill piercing stonework beside the Grand Canal. And Robert Donat plays a Canadian – which Donald Sutherland is – and is renting an apartment where the furniture is hidden under dust sheets, just like the lobby of the Europa Hotel. And that speck of grit in the eye in the restaurant – straight out of *Brief Encounter*. And Julie Christie's fingers stretching out through the bars of the water gate – *The Third Man*. Or perhaps before that, Ivor Novello desperately reaching through the railings of the fence in *The Lodger*. And just look at all those solitary men – at tables, in the street, in the Bishop's palace. A Venice as sinister as Vienna. A movie echoed again in *Bad Timing*. Yes, *The Third Man*. The original ending was cut. No happy ending. In Vancouver, with Bill, Alice once saw *F for Fake*. They walked out.

# 46

Eden and after...

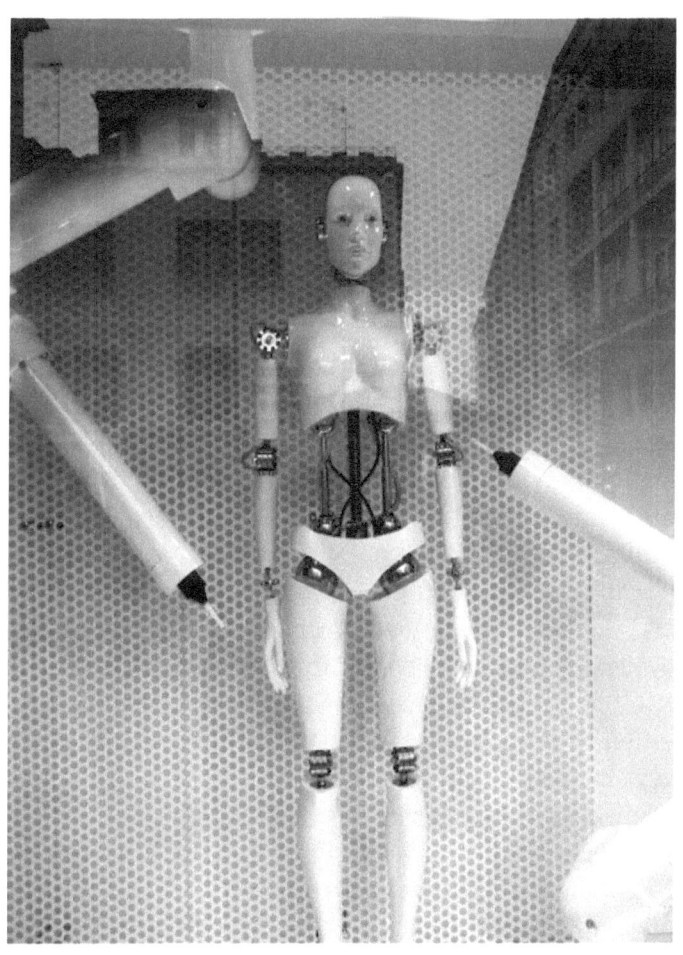

# 47

It was like. The end of a story except that. Before they turned out of. My sight her. Hand was. Through his arm — which is how. A story. Usually. Begins. Beginnings, completions. The exquisitely composed novella. Plot, characters, closure. The poetry of the thing outlived and lost and gone. Henry James arrived in Venice on 22 February 1887. He stayed seven weeks, in a gloomy apartment at the rear of Ca' Alvisi, at the mouth of the Grand Canal, opposite Santa Maria della Salute. He suffered from headaches and jaundice. He had a slight temperature and stayed in bed for sixteen days. He found his rooms insalubrious. The apartment, he grumbled, is not simpatico. Henry James disliked Venice. He grumbled about its glutinous malodorous damp. He left by train for Florence. There he wrote his Venice novella, *The Aspern Papers*. It originated in a meeting with the Countess Gamba, who owned many letters written by Byron. Some were shocking and unprintable. One, she said, was so disgusting she had burned it. After this meeting Henry James was told that Byron's mistress Claire Clairmont had lived in Florence until her death in 1879. That was not quite her real name. She had in her possession manuscripts by Shelley and Byron. Her lodger in those days was a Boston sea-captain named Silsbee. He was passionate about Shelley. Visitors reported that Captain Silsbee would sit in an armchair looking like some deep-sea monster on a Bernini fountain. He stared at the carpet and quoted Shelley with a trumpet-like twang. The quotations were quite without relevance to the conversation. Captain Silsbee was desperate to see the material which Claire Clairmont held but she always refused to show it to him. When she died the manuscripts became the possession of her niece, a single woman of about fifty. The niece knew Captain Silsbee well. His charms were rugged ones. The Shelley-crazy captain begged her to let him see this unpublished material at last. "I will give you all the letters if you will marry me," she replied. Long had her loins yearned for him. Captain Silsbee declined this exchange. He left Florence and was last heard of living inside a massive Henry James biography. HJ might have titled his novella *Death in Venice*. It is set in a dilapidated old palace on an out-of-the-way canal. It is about three deaths, really. The death, at the end, of Juliana Bordereau – the old frail woman still in possession of unpublished love letters sent to her in her youth by the long dead poet Jeffrey Aspern. The death of the heart – or at any rate of the last hopes of Miss Tita, Juliana's niece and companion, for romance and marriage. The death of the narrator's dream of getting hold of explosive and unknown manuscripts about Jeffrey Aspern's great passion. Delicately plotted and set against exquisite descriptions of Venice. And the sex! It takes just five minutes for the narrator to get Miss Tita (titter!) to the Grand Canal. She muttered a moan of ecstasy. We floated long and far. The gondola moved with slow strokes, to give her time to enjoy it. We passed into a narrow canal. When I asked her how long it was since she had come in a boat she answered: Oh, I don't know; a long time. And afterwards, a curious weariness, a sudden lapse into gloom. Her face had the flush of a sort of wounded surprise. HJ sends his narrator to the equestrian statue of Bartolomeo Colleoni. It doesn't feature in *Don't Look Now*. Alice must have passed it on the way to the isle of the dead, but she didn't notice. Venice is full of statues of historical and mythic figures. The most apt, of course, is the book-shitter.

# 48

"Life is a love story – and a horror story." What went on in that Venetian honeymoon chamber between John Cross, 40, and George Eliot, 60? He was nervous; agitated; afraid. He was depressed. He suffered from a loss of appetite. He was trembling like a jelly. His penis hung slack, uninterested. It did not wish to go on a dark, mysterious, greasy, terrifying journey into the raw unknown. To the mouth of horror! Prawn lips, shining in the candlelight. Yes, marriage to a literary celebrity is one thing. But then there is the other thing. A highly sexed wife's boiling desires. Sweet Christ have mercy! John Cross might almost have been HJ's narrator, having, in another life, taken the plunge, purely in order to obtain those precious priceless relics. And taking the plunge requires another sort of plunge. But, oh, oh, oh say again, the horror of it! Magnificently ugly, she was, old George Eliot. So cool and cruel HJ famously said. Deliciously hideous. Repellent. How she drew the adjectives from HJ's dripping, virile, burning quill! She was exceedingly plain. She had an aggressive jaw and evasive blue eyes. She had a vast pendulous nose. She had a sallow unhealthy face. Her skin was yellowish, her hair mousy. She had a low forehead and bad teeth. She looked like a horse. As for her frame, without vestments. Can you even begin to imagine? The thin, waxy, starved-looking breasts. Those dark nipples eyeing John Cross with reproach. As for the infernal regions... It was like something out of a limestone zone. A crevice rich with jostling growth. As welcoming as a prickly clump of gorse at dusk. You would not wish to insert a finger there, let alone your delicate vulnerable tranquil somnolent organ of generation. And so this is why he stands there – not standing. Forlorn, impotent, aghast, stricken with shame. His bowels begin to boil. His bladder begins to ache. His nostrils flinch and contract. He can smell her from the other side of the room. Her presence is like a shower of sour stinging rain. It is like being on the lip of a volcano – or how he imagines it must surely be. Vesuvius, say. The thick advancing waves of heat. The bubbling cauldron. Her extraordinary and grotesque lust – her greed – in one so old – sagging sixty, for sweet Christ's sake! He can feel painfully like hot pins her shimmering desire. Even from this shred of carpet – from where he coldly, shiveringly stands. Quick! *Sempre diretto!* The balcony, the velvet smooth Adriatic air, the dark water below. Splosh! Into that grandeur. And then the humiliating rescue, gabbling Italians, the aftermath of cold conversations, apologies, silences, disappointments, ailments, depression, the return to England, death. Death – but not in Venice. Death, from a kidney ailment. A miserable absurd end. This infamous tantalising episode occurred at The Europa. Which is the name of the hotel where John Baxter and Mrs Laura Baxter stay. "You know an awful lot about George Eliot and Henry James," Alice says. "For a Frenchman." Alain shakes his head. "I said nothing," he retorts. Wide-eyed, Alice asks: "Then who is responsible for this chapter?" "You're crazy as hell!" "Births. Marriages. Deaths." "Disorientated by the absence of logic in this inexorable sequence of events." "I felt now as I must tell her that I had given her an invented name." "Oh, Alain." He sits motionless, looking at a fluted white pillar in the corner. She slowly begins setting out the pieces for a new game. It is time for a Fantasio. Combine all ingredients in a mixing glass and stir well. "Perhaps you don't choose good subjects." "George Lazenby." "Venice!" "We have all the time in..." "This was a film without a script." "My mind is as empty as a vaporetta landing stage, late at night."

# 49

Alice wonders: what did Nic Roeg read about Venice, beforehand? Did he dip into James Morris's book? First published in 1960. A section deals with the sculptured lions of Venice. *The most unassuming stands on a pillar outside San Nicolò dei Mendicoli; he holds the book of St Mark in his paws, but has never presumed to apply for the wings.* This pillar is where the weird sisters are seen for a second time in the film. They stand between the pillar and a tree, as if in a strange pastiche of the twin columns of Piazzetta San Marco. Alice sees that the pillar is still there, in the same place. But the background has changed, marginally. Now there is a bench and a lighting column behind where the sisters stood. And the wall of the canal behind them and the fencing have changed in small ways. But these differences are small. It's a grey day and Alice feels as if she's wandered into Roeg's film, with everyone having just left the scene.

# 50

On the same page James Morris wrote about the silliest lion in Venice. This is the one seen in the background as Julie Christie walks by with the two sisters and the blind one says "Yes, of course. Of course! He has the gift." This lion was once located on the façade of the Accademia. *Minerva is riding this footling beast side-saddle, and on her helmet is perched another anatomical curiosity – an owl with knees.*

# 51

*Sempre diretto!* Alain ruefully confesses he is none of
those things. He is an academic – France's leading
expert on Henry Fielding. "You have seen motion image
film *The Romantic Englishwoman*?" Alice has not. And
she hasn't read *A Journey from This World to the Next*.
Alain is a huge fan. The text is presented not simply as a
satirical narrative but also as a learned edition of itself,
based on a defective manuscript, with gaps and the lack
of a conclusive ending. The manuscript, the narrator
explains, was rejected on the grounds that it was not
possible to understand it. *A Journey from This World to
the Next* consists of three sections: the narrator's death
and his journey into the next world, a description of the
transmigrations of Julian the Apostate before he was
permitted to enter Elysium, and, finally, the story of
Anne Boleyn. It is told by her spirit. This final section
has long been regarded, to quote one learned professor,
as "a rather feeble, novelettish piece of writing", leading
to the obvious conclusion that it must have been written
by a woman – quite possibly Fielding's sister Sarah.
"Doesn't it make you feel kind of mean?" Alice says. Her
voice is husky and low. Alain stares at her empty glove.
Alice is twisting it between her fingers. "He's aching to,"
she says. Alain frowns. He shrugs. He shudders. He
yawns. "Men move from desire to desire, from anguish
to anguish, from ecstasy to ecstasy, from disappointment to disappointment, from regret to regret, from
forgetfulness to forgetfulness, until at last –" "Don't be a

goof. Don't make me shoot. I will, you know." She is standing a little behind him, to one side. He has a wife and three children. He is a charming liar. Alice remembers that book by Emmanuel Carrère. You never know who anyone is. "Follow me, please." "You know nothing about literature." "What are you trying to pull?" "A jocular and flamboyantly perverted narrative." "Hey, is anybody out there?" "It all takes place on earth, most terrible of planets." "Okay. I've got a curious twisted mind like yours, so I know what you're talking about." "They were yarns too, of course." "I suspect that meaninglessness is director Roeg's quite deliberate message." BANG!

# 52

*Sempre diretto!* Found, unfinished. "You know the drill."
Brief dialogues, quotations. "Let's get some air." *Ven.*
*Diary.* "Wild rose, mad with love." *Ven. Adventure.*
"Scorpio." *Ven. Experience.* "You don't miss any angles."
The impure, the fragmented. The hammering and the
voices and the barking dog grew fainter... "Then why
shouldn't you tell me?" A stream of – "You're simply
terrific." Allusions to various – "How have I inspired you
this time?" Brief dialogues. "I finished my sentence."
"Sorry, punk." "Do you always talk like this?" "Strange. I
wasn't expecting anyone." "The Cantos consist of many
surfaces, presented with great exactitude, but with
nothing behind them." "Was that what you were looking
for?" "A single, high-powered rifle, plus sights, in a
golfing bag." "I suppose you think that suits my style?"
"It's not yet ten o'clock. There's plenty of time." "No."
"Splintered editing." "Maybe yes, maybe no." "Yes."
"What an experience!" "If you lose an hour, no one ever
finds it again." "Are five nights warmer than one night,
then?" "It is not just any kind of memory." "And are
never allowed to settle." "Venetian blind." "I thought this
was... Isn't this the place where..."

# 53

November. She has come here alone, remained alone, seen all the locations she can manage, on a trip like this. It's over. You can't see everything. There are some locations not even the fan websites mention. The building used for the police station interiors, for example. The building – perhaps the same building – used for the Bishop's palace. And at Palazzo Grimani she went as far as you are permitted to go. Some doors are locked and cannot be opened. And what happens – has happened – even in this hotel room – can never be known.

# 54

City of steps. And see! There they are. The very steps up which John Baxter – Donald Sutherland – runs in pursuit of the scampering little red figure with the pixie-hood. Those steps. Alice wonders if there are thirty-nine of them.

# 55

On her final day in Venice Alice goes to the isle of the dead. It is drenched in mist as she approaches.

# 56

When the vaporetto stops, no one else gets off. She walks alone inside a massive silence. Signs point the way to the celebrity graves. Ezra and Olga aren't too hard to find. *Click!*

# 57

On her last day in the city they meet by chance, near the graves of Ezra Pound and Olga Rudge. Alain has black curly hair, a trim moustache. Normally she does not like men with moustaches. But Alain is, apart from that facial blemish, stunningly handsome. Slim, smart-casual, amusing. Thirtyish. Twinkly eyes. Cultured. He could have been a fashion model. Alice has gone there purely for Pound. He has gone there only for Brodsky. Two worshippers. This section of the cemetery is deserted. There's just the two of them here. Alain does not like Pound's work but he adores the Russian's. As they wait for the return ferry they talk some more. She is not so sure about cinema but she approves his taste in fiction and, to some extent, poetry. Later, having crossed the fogged stretch of water, they go for a drink. She has vermouth on the rocks. He has a brandy old-fashioned. Their blood is hot, seamed with desire. But Alice feels detached. She is in no mood for a last-minute new adventure. Besides, Alain winks and says she seems ten feet tall. She is tired of men who do that, thinking they are the first, and that she will be charmed and delighted by their wit. He asks where she is staying. She avoids giving him the hotel name. Oh, over by the Grand Canal... She is expert at keeping things vague. Alain wears a silver wrist-bracelet. This is another negative. Too Essex. Plus the skin of his forearm is dense with black hair. Alice does not like men who, naked, resemble apes. And she notices that there is the edge of a curving patch of blue skin there, a tattoo. Alice Short does not like men with heavily tattooed arms or legs. They repel her. After one drink she firmly says goodbye. He is reluctant to let her go. His bubbly Parisian charm is not used to rebuffs. He wants to escort her back to the other side of the island. He says he knows Venice very well. Vair well indidd! She declines. She shakes her head. She exudes negativity. This is not a game. *Non*. No. *No*. Goodbye. On the flight homeward, looking out of the window, Alice notices a land mass protruding from an ocean of soft cloud. She presses her lens against the scratched surface. *Click!* She puts her camera away and clamps her noise-cancelling headphones to her head. All the tracks from *Red* are on her player. After that she lies back, closes her eyes. Her finger presses down on her favourite option: random shuffle.

THE END